THE RIDDLE

The questions for Miss Know It All came and went, faster and faster.

"How far away is the sun?"

"Ninety-three million miles."

"How many legs does an insect have?"

"Six."

"How do you make invisible ink?"

"With baking soda and lemon juice."

Miss Know It All knew everything. She knew how fast a bee flies and she knew how many freckles Mary had. She knew everything . . . until little Tatty stepped forward.

"What," Tatty said, "is the largest room in the world?"

Miss Know It All opened her mouth, and then closed it again slowly. She stared at Tatty and Tatty stared back at her. Miss Know It All opened her mouth a second time, and closed it once more. And then she said:

"I don't know."

MISS KNOW IT ALL

by Carol Beach York

Illustrated by Victoria de Larrea

A BANTAM SKYLARK BOOK®
TORONTO · NEW YORK · LONDON · SYDNEY · AUCKLAND

For Mother, as always

*This low-priced Bantam Book
has been completely reset in a typeface
designed for easy reading, and was printed
from new plates. It contains the complete
text of the original hard-cover edition.*
NOT ONE WORD HAS BEEN OMITTED.

RL 4, 008–012

MISS KNOW IT ALL
*A Bantam Book / published by arrangement with
the Author*

PRINTING HISTORY
*First published in the United States by Franklin Watts Inc.
of New York*
*First edition in the United Kingdom by Chatto,
Boyd & Oliver*
Bantam Skylark edition / February 1985

ISBN 0-553-15292-0

Published simultaneously in the United States and Canada

---

*Bantam Books are published by Bantam Books, Inc. Its trade-
mark, consisting of the words "Bantam Books" and the por-
trayal of a rooster, is Registered in U.S. Patent and Trademark
Office and in other countries. Marca Registrada. Bantam
Books, Inc. 666 Fifth Avenue, New York, New York 10103.*

PRINTED IN THE UNITED STATES OF AMERICA

CW   0 9 8 7 6 5 4

Contents

A Note from the Author

At Number 18 Butterfield Square stands The Good Day—home to twenty-eight little girls in dark blue dresses with white collars. Here you will meet Miss Plum and Miss Lavender, the ladies in charge. Miss Plum is wise and kind, and Miss Lavender, with her bouncing white curls, is inclined to be soft-hearted and fluttery. Cook is always busy in the kitchen baking good things to eat. You will meet Mr. Not So Much, whose monthly visits to The Good Day are dreaded by every one of the twenty-eight little girls.

You will also meet a fascinating and mysterious person . . . *Miss Know It All*.

1

The Visitor

It was a lovely bright spring day in Butterfield Square. The grass was poking out in all the front gardens of the old brick houses facing each other round the square. The crocuses were in bloom. A fresh, wonderful, anything-may-happen feeling was in the air, and everyone in the street seemed to walk with an especially lively step, as though they were hurrying to extra-nice things on this extra-nice day.

At Number 18 Butterfield Square, which was *The Good Day Home for Girls*, Cook was in the kitchen baking gingerbread biscuits and singing *O Sole Mio*. "*O sole mio*," she sang, "*la da da da*."

In the parlor, Miss Lavender and Miss Plum were enjoying the afternoon by giving themselves a concert on the violin and piano. Miss Lavender and Miss Plum were the ladies who took care of The Good Day girls. Miss Lavender was short and plump, and Miss Plum was tall and thin. Miss Lavender wore ruffly dresses and a pile of white curls on her head. Miss Plum always held herself very stiff and straight, as if she had a ruler down her back and a book balanced on the bun of her grey hair on the top of her head. Sometimes Miss Plum pinned a small brooch on the front of her dress; but she did not have any dresses with ruffles.

The ladies were alone in the parlor because the girls were all at school for the afternoon. It was Tuesday, and Tuesday was Miss Lavender's and Miss Plum's day to practice their music. End-of-the-month bills lay waiting Miss Plum's attention on the table, and Miss Lavender's mending basket was on the sofa. But all these things were forgotten as Miss Lavender tuned her violin on an *A* and Miss Plum sat down and rustled among the piano books.

A cluster of spring flowers had been put into a vase on the table. A long stream of sunlight fell across the flowers and glistened on the green leaves. It just did not seem possible that there had ever ever in the world been such a thing as a snowy day or a bitter wind!

But Miss Lavender and Miss Plum had not played very long before they heard a knock at the front door. Miss Lavender paused, bow in midair; Miss Plum's fingers stopped, poised above the keys for a tonic chord.

Miss Lavender said, "I'll go," and bow and violin in hand, she went down the hall to the big front door.

Outside, adjusting her hat against the gusts of the spring breeze, a small, round-cheeked lady waited for her knock to be answered. In one hand she carried a black patent-leather pocketbook as shiny as new shoes. In the other hand she held a small rectangular white card. When the door opened she met Miss Lavender eye to eye, for they were of an exact height. Miss Lavender peered out from under her pile of white curls. The caller held out the small white card.

"My card," she said.

"Oh," said Miss Lavender. She shifted her bow to the hand that held the violin. Then she took the card. And read:

MISS KNOW IT ALL
Geography History Arithmetic
Science Spelling
Recipes, Riddles and Weather Reports
Reasonable Rates

Before Miss Lavender could say anything, Miss Know It All had stepped into the hall and was taking off her hat.

"Pay no attention to that last part," she said, "—the reasonable rates. I'm going to give you a free demonstration."

"A free demonstration?" Miss Lavender said.

"A free demonstration," Miss Know It All repeated. "I give them now and then—good advertising, you know." She sniffed a deep sniff of the gingerbread biscuits baking in the kitchen. Then she looked round with approval at the long sunny hallway in which she was standing.

Miss Plum had come to the parlor doorway to see what was happening. She stood as straight and proper as ever—very calm, very efficient.

"What is it, Miss Lavender?" she asked, and came along the hall towards the visitor.

"I—I'm not quite sure," Miss Lavender said. She handed the small rectangular white card to Miss Plum. Miss Plum would know what to do.

"Ladies," Miss Know It All said, in an elegant tone, "you have been selected as the fortunate people to receive a free demonstration. Fully, wholly, entirely, unconditionally and positively without charge. Free."

"A demonstration of what?" Miss Lavender looked more confused than ever. Even Miss Plum, who by now had had a chance to read the little white card for herself, did not look exactly sure of what was happening.

"A demonstration of my remarkable powers," said Miss Know It All. "My name was not just pulled out of a hat, you know. My sun and stars, no! It means just what it says. Ask me something—quick, quick, quick!" She snapped her fingers as fast as she spoke, but Miss Lavender and

Miss Plum were so taken aback by her sudden demand to be asked something, that they could not think of anything to ask.

"Come, come," Miss Know It All chided. "There must be something you want to know. Ask me anything."

"What comes after *Pussy cat, pussy cat, where have you been?*" Miss Plum asked. It was the first thing that came to her mind, and she thought it was rather good.

"I've been to London, to visit the queen!" Miss Know It All said at once. She snapped out the answer almost before Miss Plum had finished asking the question.

Miss Plum and Miss Lavender looked at each other, trying to think of something harder than that to ask.

"How fast can a bee fly?" said Miss Lavender.

"The average cruising speed of the honeybee is thirteen miles per hour," replied Miss Know It All without a moment's hesitation. Then for good measure she added, "And a bee's wing-beat may be fifteen thousand times a minute."

"Ohhh," said Miss Lavender with considerable awe. She and Miss Plum looked at each other again, and Miss Know It All made herself so far at home as to walk on down the hall towards the parlor. Miss Plum and Miss Lavender collected themselves at last, and followed her.

"Ah!" said Miss Know It All, at the parlor doorway. "A lovely room. Shall we go in and sit down?"

Miss Plum said, "Yes—I suppose so——" and followed Miss Know It All into the parlor. Miss Lavender came last of all, still not quite sure what was going on, and still marvelling at bees' wings beating fifteen thousand times a minute. She sat down in the first chair she came to, not even realizing that she was still holding her violin and bow.

"You see, ladies," Miss Know It All explained sweetly, "I go all over the world answering questions for people."

"Is that so?" said Miss Plum rather suspiciously. She had never heard of such a thing.

"You must be very smart," said Miss Lavender with admiration. "I suppose you spend a great deal of time studying."

"But that's just it," said Miss Know It All. "I

16

hardly have to study at all. I just know everything already. It's a knack." She paused a moment, and then said, "Surely you've known people like that before?"

Miss Plum could not help smiling. "I expect we've all known some people who *thought* they knew everything."

Miss Lavender nodded. "Everybody knows someone like that," she agreed.

"But there's one difference," Miss Know It All said with a wag of one finger. "I really do know everything; the others just think they do."

"How true," murmured Miss Lavender— who was just now recalling a cousin of hers who always thought he knew everything.

"I was walking along," Miss Know It All continued, "thinking to myself that it was about time for a free demonstration to some lucky household, when I saw your sign out by the gate. And I thought to myself, Here's just the place. So here I am, ready to demonstrate."

"Well, that's very nice of you," Miss Plum said, still somewhat suspicious of this strange visitor. "But are you quite sure it's really free? You see, we have a very careful budget here, and I'm afraid we have no allowance left over for extras this month."

"Perfectly, absolutely, completely, unquestionably, indisputably and totally free," Miss Know It All declared.

Miss Lavender and Miss Plum exchanged glances. Miss Know It All really did seem to mean that it was not going to cost them anything.

"Now, where are the little girls?" Miss Know It All asked. She settled herself comfortably on the sofa and crossed her feet at the ankles in a ladylike manner.

"They will be along soon," Miss Plum said. The clock on the mantle pointed to five minutes past three. "They go to the school in Harcourt Street, and they should be back any minute."

Even as she spoke, a line of little girls appeared round the corner of Butterfield Square. Not a neat two-by-two marching line, but a straggly running-and-skipping and playing-tag sort of line, strung out behind and filling the pavement. There were twenty-eight little girls, each with a dark blue coat and cap and long black stockings and black shoes with buckles at the side. Some carried schoolbooks for homework, and some had taken off their caps and were running along with their coats open, enjoying the warm spring afternoon.

"They'll be changing from those long stockings any day now." Miss Lavender felt that she should explain.

"Oh, I know that," Miss Know It All said, smiling gently to herself.

Miss Lavender and Miss Plum exchanged glances again. If Miss Know It All knew how fast a bee flew, she might be likely to know almost anything. Or everything!

Along the black iron railings and in at the gate came the girls, up the walk and into the front hall with a burst.

"Gingerbread biscuits!" one girl cried, and they all raced to the long hall cupboard to hang up their coats and caps. The sound in the parlor from all this activity was very great. Then past the parlor door the ladies saw all the little girls running to the kitchen for their biscuits, a thundering herd of dark blue dresses and round white collars:

tall girls, short girls, thin girls, plump girls, short hair, curly hair, pigtails and hair-bows; freckled faces and tiny noses and clean ears.

Miss Plum excused herself and stepped out of the parlor. She went back towards the kitchen to tell the girls about their visitor and the free demonstration.

Miss Lavender at last remembered her violin and bow, and put them away in the case.

Miss Know It All folded her hands, smiled serenely and waited for the questions to begin.

2

1,065,811 × 942

The twenty-eight little girls lined up in a double row along the longest parlor wall—the older girls at the back, the smallest in front. Miss Know It All had taken off her coat, and it could now be seen that she wore a dress of plain brown silk with a row of brown buttons down the front. She did not look in any way unusual. Her shiny black pocketbook rested on the floor by her feet.

She smiled at the girls and nodded with satisfaction when they were all lined up.

"We'll just go straight down the line," she said, "and everyone can ask a question. A spelling word or a history date, a riddle or an arithmetic

problem—whatever you like. See if you can catch me; find something I don't know. You never will."

"What if we do?" Miss Plum asked.

"Oh, that never happens." Miss Know It All shook her head and waved her hand airily.

Miss Plum was not sure this was exactly an answer, but she sat back in her chair and nodded for the children to begin. They did not seem burst-

ing with questions, so to get things started Miss Lavender said, "What King of England did King James VI of Scotland become?"

"*King James I: 1603 to 1625*," replied Miss Know It All without batting an eye.

"Now go ahead, girls," Miss Lavender coaxed. "Start there in the back row, with the big girls."

The first girl in the back row was Elsie May, who was twelve, the oldest girl of all. She had two long yellow braids. She was very vain about them and kept them tied with satin ribbon, when she could find it.

"What is 1,065,811 × 942?" asked Elsie May, and all the girls turned and stared at her. It did not seem a very fair question to them.

Elsie May stuck her nose up in the air, and waited.

But she did not have to wait long. Miss Know It All shut her eyes tight for a moment, giving the impression that all those numbers were springing up into view before her in the dark of her closed eyes.

Popping her eyes open, she smiled and said, "1,003,993,962."

There was a pause—because now that it came down to it, nobody knew if that was right or not.

"You may get a paper and sit at my table and see if that is correct," Miss Plum said to Elsie May. So Elsie May had to write down the whole problem to check Miss Know It All's answer, and she soon felt very sorry indeed that she had asked such a silly thing.

The next girl in line asked in what year the Pilgrims had sailed from Plymouth to America in their ship *The Mayflower*.

> *"The Mayflower sailed in 1620,*
> *Carrying on board Pilgrims plenty."*

said Miss Know It All. She didn't have to think a second about that one.

The girl who asked that question knew the answer was right. Her class at school had just that day been studying about the Pilgrims.

And after that the questions and answers came so fast that nobody bothered to stop and check. Each girl was eager for her turn, now that she saw what the game was like. Some of the answers the girls already knew before they asked. As for the others, there was something about the way Miss Know It All gave her answers that had an authoritative ring, as though she were just that minute reading them out of the encyclopedia.

When she said that the rainfall in Panama averaged 140 inches a year, and that the population of Iceland was 190,000, everyone felt that she was surely right. Even Miss Plum.

On and on the questions and answers went—faster and faster.

"How far away is the sun?"

"Ninety-three million miles."

"How many legs does an insect have?"

"Six."

"Who invented the telephone?"

"Alexander Graham Bell: 1876."

"How much water can a camel drink?"

"Enough to last for three days."

"What makes thunder?"

"The sudden expansion of the air in the path of a discharge of atmospheric electricity from cloud to cloud or cloud to earth."

No one said anything for a minute after that.

Then: "Spell Llanfairfechan."

"L-l-a-n-f-a-i-r-f-e-c-h-a-n."

"How do you make invisible ink?"

"With baking soda and lemon juice."

26

"How can you tell when a Christmas cake is done?"

"Test it with a silver knife."

"What is the shape of a hummingbird's nest?"

"Thimble-shaped."

Little Ann, the very smallest girl of all, only five and a half years old, was the first to ask a riddle. When it came to her turn, she said, "What has four legs and only one foot?"

And Miss Know It All answered, *"A bed."*

Mary, next in line after Little Ann, tried to think of a harder riddle than that. She had just thought of one, but had not said it yet, when a loud knock was heard at the front door.

As though the knock jogged their memories, Miss Plum and Miss Lavender clapped their hands to their faces with dismay. *That* loud knock could only be Mr. Not So Much.

And they had forgotten it was his day!

3

Mr. Not So Much

Mr. Not So Much strode down the hall, stiff and thin and dressed all in black. He carried his hat in his hand, but did not at once remove his gloves.

He stood in the parlor doorway looking sternly at the scene before him: at Miss Know It All sitting so primly on the sofa; the twenty-eight little girls lined up along the wall. He was sure that whatever was going on was probably not good.

"This is Mr. Not So Much," Miss Plum explained to Miss Know It All.

Miss Know It All smiled cheerfully and said, "How do you do?"

28

Mr. Not So Much nodded suspiciously.

"Mr. Not So Much is one of the directors of The Good Day," Miss Lavender said. "He comes one afternoon a month to—to see how we are." (She had hesitated because Mr. Not So Much really came to see that Miss Lavender and Miss Plum were not spending too much money on anything—but that did not seem quite the right thing to say.)

"How nice," Miss Know It All said. Miss Lavender and Miss Plum of course had quite another opinion of the matter.

All the children were afraid of Mr. Not So Much. He always came and told Miss Lavender and Miss Plum things like:

"Not so much chocolate in Christmas stockings."

"Not so much wood on the fire."

"Not so much electricity burning."

Then he would say, "A penny saved is a penny earned."

Or: "Waste not, want not."

Sometimes he said: "Not so much noise."

"Not so much running."

"Not so much jumping."

"Not so much playing."

"Not so much laughing."

"Not so much coughing."

"Not so much sneezing."

"Not so much fidgeting."

"Not so much shuffling."

And once he had said, "Not so much breathing"—although no one could remember why.

"This is Miss Know It All," Miss Plum said to Mr. Not So Much. "She is giving us a *free* demonstration of her amazing powers."

"Yes—*free*," said Miss Lavender.

Mr. Not So Much looked as fierce as ever, and Miss Lavender hastened to add, "She really does know everything—absolutely *every*thing."

Mr. Not So Much snorted. He drew off his gloves at last and held them tight in one hard bony old hand. His forehead wrinkled up with disapproval. He was not sure anything in the world was really free.

"Yes, indeed," Miss Lavender rattled on, somewhat flustered. She was used to Mr. Not So

Much, but she was afraid that Miss Know It All would be startled to meet someone so fearsome and cross. "She has told us the population of Iceland and how fast a bee flies—not only that, but how fast his wings go. Fifteen thousand times a minute, Mr. Not So Much; just think of *that*!"

Mr. Not So Much did not look any less fierce.

Miss Lavender tried desperately to recall some of the other answers that Miss Know It All had given. Her eyes fell upon Little Ann, and she exclaimed:

"Oh, yes—she told us what has four heads and only one leg. Or something——" The riddle did not sound just right, that way. Some of the girls began to giggle.

Mr. Not So Much only said, "Not so much foolishness, not so much foolishness."

Then he glowered at the girls and said, "Not so much tittering."

The girls stared back, gulping down their laughter. Surely "tittering" was the funniest word they had ever heard!

Mr. Not So Much did not seem to think it was a funny word, however; nor did he seem to be particularly pleased to meet Miss Know It All, amazing as she was.

"How do you do, madam," he said without a smile.

Then he laid his gloves in his hat elegantly, and said to Miss Plum, "I have only a moment today." Which everyone thought was fortunate.

Mr. Not So Much and Miss Plum went aside to Miss Plum's table, where Elsie May had left a clutter of paper from working out $1,065,811 \times 942$. Together they considered some of the month's bills that Miss Plum found under the arithmetic papers.

The room was very still. Every once in a while the others could hear Mr. Not So Much saying, "Not so much—not so much——" as he looked over the costs for feeding and clothing and taking care of twenty-eight little girls.

However, he was finally finished, and casting an eye about the room one last time, he said, "Not so much water in those vases," and stalked away down the hall.

When the door had closed behind him, everyone breathed a sigh of relief, and Mary—

standing next to Little Ann—burst out at once:

"What has teeth, but can't eat?"

She had been waiting all the time to ask her riddle!

"*A comb*," said Miss Know It All. She smiled at Mary, who could certainly have used a comb at that moment for her tangled red curls.

Then, next to Mary, Miss Know It All saw another little girl—not quite as big as Mary, who was nearly nine, but bigger than Little Ann, who was only five and a half. The little girl's hair fell across her forehead into her eyes. She looked as if she could use a comb even more than Mary. Her name was Tatty. For a moment Miss Know It All hesitated. Her eyes met Tatty's eyes peering out from under the straggling hair.

Miss Plum and Miss Lavender waited. All the girls waited.

At last Miss Know It All said slowly, "All right—next question, please."

"What is the largest room in the world?" said Tatty.

The parlor was very still. The girls waited. Miss Lavender and Miss Plum waited. Miss Know

It All opened her mouth, and then closed it again slowly. She stared at Tatty and Tatty stared back at her. Miss Know It All opened her mouth a second time, and closed it once more. And then she said:

"*I don't know.*"

4

The Riddle

For a moment it seemed that everything stopped. It seemed that the spring wind stopped blowing and the earth stopped turning round the sun. It seemed that the clock stopped ticking, and that nothing moved anywhere; and then, softly—*ticktock, ticktock, ticktock*—the clock could be heard ticking after all.

"Well, my word," Miss Lavender said, making little sounds in her throat. She coughed politely and smiled uncertainly at Miss Know It All. Miss Know It All sat silent and stunned. She opened her mouth once or twice and closed it again, and then she said a second time: "I don't know."

All the little girls nudged each other and began to fidget and whisper. Miss Plum finally stood up and clapped her hands for attention.

"Now, now, girls. Quiet, please," she said. Then she turned to Miss Know It All. "Take your time. Think about it. Maybe you'll get the answer."

Miss Know It All at last seemed to be getting over her shock. She shook her head and even began to smile a little to herself. "No, I just don't know." Slowly she began to put on her coat. "I don't expect you're going to think very much of my demonstration," she said.

"Why, it was wonderful," Miss Lavender assured her. "Just wonderful. Fancy knowing all those things."

Everyone agreed that Miss Know It All was wonderful, and she was grateful for their praise. But finally she said, "I think you'll have to tell us, Tatty. So that I can be on my way."

Everyone looked at Tatty—and when Tatty

did not say anything, Miss Plum prodded her. "All right, Tatty, tell us the answer to the riddle. What is the largest room in the world?"

"I don't know," Tatty said. "I wanted her to tell me."

Miss Know It All began to unbutton her coat.

"I can't be on my way until every question is correctly answered," she said. "It's one of my rules."

Everyone looked at her, but she only shrugged her shoulders helplessly and went on unbuttoning her coat. "You wouldn't want me to break one of my own rules?"

"No, of course not," Miss Plum and Miss Lavender murmured. They looked across at each other. They were not sure just how long Miss Know It All intended to stay—or where she would sleep, for they did not have an extra bed in all the house.

"Tatty," Miss Plum said, "who ever heard of asking a riddle when you don't even know the answer?"

The other girls looked at Tatty as though *any-one* would have known better than *that*!

Little Ann said, "What is lighter than a feather but harder to hold?"—but no one listened to her. Everyone wanted to know why Tatty had asked a riddle when she did not know the answer. It was one thing to ask Miss Know It All a question about geography or arithmetic without knowing the answer yourself. But it was something else to ask a riddle. When you asked a riddle, you already knew the answer. Everyone knew that.

Poor Tatty squirmed under so much attention. Her long stockings were sagging, and her fingers were not very clean. Her hair fell in her eyes, though she tried to brush it back; and whenever she looked out past it she saw that everyone else was still watching her, waiting for her to say something.

At last Tatty said, "One day I heard some big boys talking, when I was on my way to school. They were walking just in front of me. One of them was asking riddles. He said, 'What do you lose every time you stand up?' And the other boy said, 'Your lap.' Then the boy said, 'What has three—'"

"Never mind all that," Miss Plum interrupted. "What about the largest room in the world?"

"W—ell," said Tatty, drawing out the word as long as she could, "one of them asked that riddle, but just then we came to the school gate, and I stopped, and the boys went on down the street before I heard the answer."

Miss Plum snapped her mouth shut and closed her eyes dramatically. Her expression clearly indicated that she had never heard of such a thing in her life!

Miss Lavender began to fuss and flutter and wave her hands. "Now, isn't that just too bad," she said. "Isn't that just too bad."

Meantime Miss Know It All had again tried to think of the answer.

"I just *can't* seem to get that one," she complained at last. "I'll give it up for now, I suppose."

She patted the sofa cushions and said, "Don't worry about a bed for me. This sofa is very comfy, and I can sleep here. It will do splendidly."

5

Mean Elsie May

One by one the days passed.

Cook made apple dumplings for supper one night. And butterscotch pudding the next night. And coconut trifle the night after that.

Every morning the little girls got up and washed and dressed and made their beds and tidied their rooms and ate their oatmeal (sometimes it was oatmeal-with-raisins) and went to school.

Every afternoon they came hurrying back, running in the spring sunshine.

And all the time Miss Know It All stayed. She slept on the sofa at night, and during the day she sat in the parlor and tried to find the answer to Tatty's question.

Miss Plum went to the local library and brought home all the books on riddles that she could find: four. And then the ladies, Miss Plum and Miss Lavender and Miss Know It All, read through the books to see if any had the riddle, "What is the largest room in the world?" Cook could hear them laughing and asking each other riddles as they went through the books. But in the end Miss Plum closed them all up and carried them back to the library. Not one had anything about the largest room in the world.

Then Miss Know It All began to write down all the things she knew as fast as she could think of them—just in case that way the answer might pop into her head after all. She sat at Miss Plum's big table by the windows and wrote and wrote and wrote, until everything in the parlor was covered with sheets of paper filled with all the things that Miss Know It All knew. The little girls tried to think what the answer might be. They asked their teachers at school, and all the children there. But no one knew. Cook asked everyone she saw: the milkman and the butcher and the baker, the grocer and the greengrocer, and all her friends and relatives. But not one of them knew, either.

Time went by. The days grew warmer and warmer. The little girls stopped wearing their long black stockings and began to wear short white ankle socks. Soon the lilac and the laburnum would be in bloom.

"I think I shall have to stay forever," Miss Know It All said one night at suppertime. She pretended to laugh about that, but there was a sound of sadness behind the laughter, and everyone was quiet for a moment.

"You mustn't worry," Miss Lavender said kindly. "We're very happy to have you here. You are the most amazing person we've ever known. Isn't that right, Miss Plum?"

"Yes," Miss Plum said. "That is certainly right."

Miss Know It All seemed to brighten up. She said, "As long as I'm here, you may ask me some more questions if you like. I don't want to get out of practice."

So after supper that night everyone had a

turn asking Miss Know It All a question. And she answered every one.

"Who discovered America?"

> *"Christopher Columbus sailed away,*
> *And found America one day."*

"What is the highest mountain in the world?"
"Mount Everest, 29,028 feet."
"How long is the Amazon River?"
"Thirty-nine hundred miles."
"What is it which everyone has seen, but will never see again?"
"Yesterday."
"Where is the driest spot in the world?"
"It is said to be the Atacama Desert in Chile, where there isn't even enough rainfall to measure."
"What is the largest animal ever known?"
"The blue whale can grow to 110 feet long."
"What has an eye, but can't see at all?"
"A needle."
There was not one question that Miss Know It All could not answer.

46

One afternoon after school, Tatty and Little Ann and Mary were walking back to Butterfield Square, the very last of all the girls, when Mary said, "I wonder if Miss Know It All knows any magic? She seems to know everything else."

"Wouldn't it be exciting if she did," Tatty said.

Little Ann began to hop and clap her hands together. "Let's ask her if she will do some magic for us."

"We don't know if she can or not," Mary said, "but I'll ask her."

They ran all the rest of the way to Butterfield Square. But they were disappointed to find that Miss Know It All was taking a nap and they would have to wait until suppertime to talk to her. They went upstairs and got out their crayons and coloring books.

They had not been coloring long when two other girls, Kate and Phoebe, came along.

"We're going to ask Miss Know It All if she knows any magic," Tatty said.

"I bet she doesn't," Kate said. She was always very practical and down-to-earth about things.

47

She did not get as easily excited as Phoebe, who at once began to cry, "Yes, ask her, ask her! Wouldn't that be wonderful!"

"We can't ask her yet," Little Ann said. "She's taking a nap."

"Well, ask her as soon as she wakes up," Phoebe urged. "If she knows everything, she must know magic too."

"Just the opposite," Kate disagreed. "Magic is a thing all by itself, and if Miss Know It All knows all those other things, that's probably enough."

By and by it was suppertime, and the girls put away their crayons and coloring books. Tatty put hers on the chair by her bed.

After the girls had gone downstairs, Elsie May came along the hall, feeling very cross because she could not find pretty ribbons for her hair. She saw Tatty's crayons and coloring book in the chair, and she picked them up and hid them way back in the dark under Tatty's bed, just to play a trick on Tatty.

She was careful to be sure that no one was looking. Then she flounced away.

6

The Three Treasures

Mary had very red hair and very blue eyes, and more freckles than anyone had ever counted. Once she had asked Miss Know It All how many freckles she had, and Miss Know It All had said three hundred and eleven. So it was not likely after all that anyone ever would have to bother to count Mary's freckles.

"It's not every girl who knows to the exact number of how many freckles she has," Miss Lavender reminded Mary; and Mary was rather pleased to have three hundred and eleven. No one else at The Good Day had anywhere near so many.

As soon as she could that night at supper, Mary asked Miss Know It All if she could do magic. Tatty and Little Ann, sitting one on each side of Mary, waited eagerly for the answer. They had already decided the magic things they would ask Miss Know It All to do. Tatty was going to ask her to take them on a flying carpet, and Little Ann was going to ask her to turn the black railings outside into real sticks of licorice, so that she could have a bite every time she went past. And Mary was going to ask Miss Know It All to give her a magic wishing ring with three magic wishes.

"No," said Miss Know It All. "I do not know any magic."

There went the flying carpet and the licorice-stick railings and the magic wishing ring. Tatty and Mary and Little Ann looked so surprised; they could not think of anything to say.

"Oh," said Elsie May, sticking her nose up in the air, "what a stupid thing to ask. Magic!"

"It is not stupid," Mary said, and Miss Plum clapped her hands and said, "That's enough, girls."

Miss Know It All seemed to be thinking.

Then she said, "I don't actually do any magic, but I have a few things you might like to see."

"Magic things?" asked Tatty.

"I'll show you after supper," Miss Know It All promised, and that was all she would say until supper was over.

Then everyone went into the parlor. Miss Know It All sat down on the sofa and crossed her ankles. She asked if someone would please bring her coat, which had been hung away in the cupboard.

Mary and Tatty both ran to get it together, and bumped around and made a great to-do in the little cupboard where umbrellas were kept and also Miss Lavender's violin case. At last they brought out the coat and carried it to Miss Know It All.

Miss Know It All spread the coat on her lap and reached into one of the pockets. "I will show you three things I always carry with me when I travel. My treasures, I call them. With these, I can go anywhere in the world."

First she took out a box covered with beautiful shiny gold-foil paper. Black letters on the cover said: SUPERIOR CHOCOLATES.

Miss Know It All opened the box, and although it hardly looked as if it contained enough chocolates to go round, she handed it to the nearest girl and said, "Won't you all have a chocolate while I show you the other things?"

The girl took a chocolate, and passed the box to the next girl, who did the same. As the box went from hand to hand, Miss Know It All reached into a second coat pocket and took out a photograph in a flat, gilded frame.

"This is a photograph of my dear brother Albert. If I ever feel homesick on my travels, I have only to stop in a good light, take out my photograph, and get a smile from Albert—and then I turn it over like this and there's a neat little mirror on the back so that I can see if I'm tidy and if my hat's on straight. It's quite a travelling aid, as you can see."

She set the photograph on the tea table by the sofa for everyone to admire. From a third coat pocket she took a little silver music box. On top of the box was a tiny figure of a ballerina standing on her toes. When the music began to play, the ballerina turned round as though she were dancing to the music.

"It's *The Blue Danube Waltz*," Miss Know It All said. "When I feel in the mood for some entertainment, I take out my music box and there I have *The Blue Danube Waltz*."

All the little girls watched while the ballerina turned first one way and then the other, then all the way round in a circle. The music tinkled out like a fairy tune. They thought they could sit and watch and listen forever.

By that time, the box of chocolates had been

all round the room, to every girl and to Miss Lavender and Miss Plum. But it was still full to the brim with chocolates, as full as when Miss Know It All had first taken it out of her coat pocket.

"This, of course, comes in handy if I feel hungry," she said. "My chocs box, I call it."

She closed the cover and put the box away in her coat pocket. Then she put away the photograph of Albert, and the tiny silver music box. One by one the little girls watched the treasures going back into the coat pockets.

"With these three things, I can go anywhere in the world," Miss Know It All said, "and have everything I need." And there was not one little girl in all the room who would not have liked especially to have such a box of chocolates, for it was never empty no matter how many chocolates were taken out.

"Just look at the time!" Miss Lavender exclaimed, catching sight of the clock. "Time for bed."

"Past time," Miss Plum said. "Hurry along now, girls—it's very late."

The children were all sleepy, but they had been so interested in Miss Know It All's treasures that they had not noticed how sleepy they were getting. They wished Miss Know It All would stay forever. They hoped she never would find the answer she needed.

Slowly they climbed the stairs, yawning and rubbing their eyes. Elsie May stood in Tatty's doorway. "Where are your crayons and coloring book, Tatty?" she asked in a funny sweet voice.

"You've hidden them again!" Tatty cried. She looked helplessly at the empty chair by her bed. She felt too sleepy to start looking all over the room. Sometimes Elsie May hid things up high where no one else could reach, because she was so tall.

Elsie May began to giggle. "Aren't you going to look for your things, Tatty?"

Tatty didn't know where to start looking. She just stood and stared round the room.

"Aren't you going to look for your things?" Elsie May said again. She was sure her hiding place was so good that Tatty would never find it.

Tatty might look under the bed—but she couldn't see way back in the dark where the crayons and book were unless she looked very carefully.

Elsie May waited, twisting the end of one of her beautiful yellow braids. But Tatty did not begin to look in the closet or behind the chair or under her pillow. Instead, all of a sudden she began to smile to herself. "I don't have to look," she said. Then she turned and went back down the stairs, and Elsie May hung over the railing, furious with anger, and called after her: "Tatty is a tattletale! Tatty is a tattletale!"

Tatty did not even look back. When she was downstairs she opened the parlor door and Elsie May could hear her saying: "Miss Know It All, where are my crayons and coloring book, please?"

"Why, right under your bed, my dear," said Miss Know It All.

And Elsie May stamped her feet and ran away before Tatty came back.

7

The Answer

Then at last, quite unexpectedly, after so many days of trying to find the answer to Tatty's riddle, suddenly the answer was found.

Tatty and Mary and Little Ann found it simply by asking the most unlikely person in the world: Mr. Not So Much.

He came pounding upon the front door one rainy afternoon while the little girls were still at school. The glistening rain had turned the black iron gate and fence rails into such shiny sticks that they looked like real licorice, even without magic. Puddles had collected in the paving stones. Cars swishing by spattered anyone standing too near the curb. Passers-by bent under their umbrellas, and a grey mist hung in the air.

"This is the dreariest day I have ever seen in my life," Cook said to herself, and began to bake something extra good for supper to lift the gloom.

Miss Lavender and Miss Plum were in the parlor, and Miss Know It All was sitting at the table writing down things she knew. She had just written "A giraffe's tongue is eighteen inches long," and was starting on the principal products of Pakistan. It was the day for Mr. Not So Much's regular monthly visit, but Miss Lavender and Miss Plum did not expect him because of the rain. So no one even had a chance to worry or be nervous, before he was upon them. Because of the pouring rain he had knocked only once and then, as the door was not locked, let himself in to get more quickly out of the rain. He came down the hall and appeared like an apparition—tall and dark and scowling—in the parlor doorway.

"My goodness! Mr. Not So Much!" Miss Lavender saw him first, and she half rose from her chair before she remembered the sewing basket was in her lap—or had been. As she moved, it slid down her smooth silky skirt and turned upside down upon the carpet. Buttons and pins and spools of thread scattered every which way, and the scissors hit Miss Lavender sharply upon the toe.

Miss Plum got up hastily, in great agitation, and overturned a small footstool on which Miss Know It All had just put a stack of papers to give herself more room for writing at the table. The footstool made a thud and the papers floated off under chair legs and into corners.

Miss Know It All tried to push back her chair to get up and catch the papers, and the chair leg caught in the carpet. The whole chair overturned and Miss Know It All crashed to the floor, striking her foot against the table as she fell and upsetting a vase of flowers which jolted over the edge of the table and splashed upon the floor. The vase rolled across the carpet with flowers falling out along the way one by one, until it came to a stop against Mr. Not So Much's shoes, one last long stem dangling from its mouth.

"Everything in its usual state of confusion here, I see," Mr. Not So Much observed.

Miss Lavender scrambled to gather up the sewing things, and Miss Plum gathered up Miss Know It All—who said at once that she was not hurt one bit by the fall. "I'm right as rain, right as rain," she declared, and Mr. Not So Much gave her a very sour look just because she mentioned rain.

Then Miss Plum and Miss Know It All picked up the scattered papers and flowers, and Mr. Not So Much picked up the vase. He stood holding it with an expression of suffering, until Miss Plum rescued it from him.

"We—we—weren't expecting—you——" Miss Lavender stammered. She was stuffing thread and needles and pins into her sewing basket in a way that would take her days afterwards to straighten out.

"Not so much chatter," Mr. Not So Much said. He took off his coat and shook it. It was an extremely wet coat, and if there had been a fire burning in the fireplace he could have put it nearby to dry. As it was, the fireplace was bare. Only on very wintry days did the ladies light a fire there. They had a good furnace in the basement for heat;

the fire was only to make the parlor cheerful and cosy, and they had to be careful to make their wood last as long as possible. Today, with the chilly, misty rain, it would have been nice to have perhaps just a little fire. But there was none, and at least—Miss Plum thought as she took Mr. Not So Much's wet coat—at least he could not say, "Not so much wood, ladies," which was certainly one of his favorite speeches.

Mr. Not So Much sat down stiffly and frowned at the spots of water left on the carpet by the rolling vase. Miss Know It All was trying to blot up the spots with some of her papers.

"You remember Miss Know It All," Miss Plum said.

Mr. Not So Much nodded absently and continued to watch with his dark and burning gaze as Miss Know It All dabbed up the last of the water. Then she seemed to know it was time to make herself very quiet and inconspicuous. She had set up her overturned chair, and now she sat down very noiselessly at the table and folded her hands together on her lap.

"My—it's quite a day to be out, isn't it?" Miss

Lavender said to get the conversation started. The parlor windows were streaming with rain, and the darkening mist pressed in ever more closely upon them. It was nearly time for the children to be coming back from school, and Miss Lavender was glad to recall that the girls had all set out with raincoats and boots and every umbrella that could be found (which came out to three girls to an umbrella; not at all bad, Miss Lavender had told them).

"No—no—we certainly didn't expect you in such weather," she finished faintly. She smoothed her dress and patted the fluffy white curls which rose in a heap upon her head.

"When it's my day to come, you may count on it that I will come," Mr. Not So Much replied grimly. "I don't approve of giving in to the weather."

"You're quite right," Miss Plum agreed quickly.

"Yes, indeed." Miss Lavender seemed delighted with this thought. "You're quite right, Mr. Not So Much. Quite right—very admirable, very admirable——" But her voice trailed away and stopped because after she had said that, there did not seem to be anything else to say.

At last Mr. Not So Much rose and began to stalk about the room, looking here and there and frowning as though it was all too horrible to bear.

"Not so much paper—not so much ink," he said, when he caught sight of Miss Know It All's table. "Surely this is wasteful."

Miss Know It All trembled, but Miss Plum said right away, "Oh, no indeed, sir. We intend to use the backs of the paper too, you see."

"Ah, then," said Mr. Not So Much, "that's not so bad. A penny saved is a penny earned."

"Oh, how true, how true," Miss Lavender and Miss Plum answered together, smiling sweetly at Mr. Not So Much.

"Waste not, want not," Mr. Not So Much said.

"How true, how true," said Miss Plum, winking at Miss Lavender.

"Oh, my, yes; how true indeed," Miss Lavender answered solemnly.

Mr. Not So Much looked pleased, in his fierce way, to see that they were agreeing. "It's all a matter of economy and wisdom, ladies," he reminded them, tapping his own head to show how wise he was himself.

Then Cook brought in the tea things, and Mr. Not So Much drank a cup of tea as bitter as himself, and said, "Not so much sugar in the cakes; not so much starch in the tea cloth; not so much polish on the furniture, and not so much light in the lamps. A forty-watt bulb would do nicely here," he said, pointing to the lamp by the tea table. "In fact, we do not need this light at all." And he turned off the lamp, which left them in a dim and shadowy circle drinking their tea, for the day outside had grown steadily darker and more dreary. Miss Know It All could hardly see, and ended up stirring her tea with a butter knife.

But at last—as always—Mr. Not So Much's visit drew to a close. It would soon be over for another month. Miss Lavender and Miss Plum could go back to starching the tea cloths and turning on lamps, polishing furniture and eating cakes full of sugar. They grew very cheerful thinking about it. They were about to accompany Mr. Not So Much gaily to the door, but he said he could find it himself after all these years. He put on his coat, took up his hat, and went out of the parlor.

He was just in time to be almost run down entirely by the little girls returning from school in dripping raincoats and squishy boots.

Trying to stand out of the way, Mr. Not So Much watched with some amazement at how quickly they came tumbling into the hall, wet and noisy, and how fast they stampeded past him towards the kitchen—where they knew Cook would have something good for them to eat. Behind them in the hall they left a sea of umbrellas propped open to dry and boots lined up along the carpet edge. (All raincoats had to go straight to the kitchen to be hung up and dripped out there.)

Then when Mr. Not So Much had at last begun to pick his way through the umbrellas, growing like tilted toadstools along the hall, Tatty and Mary and Little Ann came straggling in, last of all. They shrank back against the wall when they saw Mr. Not So Much coming towards the front door, and he looked at them sternly.

"Well, lost your tongues?" he said.

"Hullo," said Mary bravely. She was the eldest of the three, and it seemed it was up to her to speak.

At the doorway, Mr. Not So Much paused and peered out into rain. There was no change, except that the mist was thicker and the puddles were deeper and the day was greyer and more cheerless than ever.

"I dare you to say something," Mary whispered to Tatty. Mary felt very proud of herself for having actually spoken to Mr. Not So Much.

"Scaredy," she said, when Tatty remained silent.

"I am not scared," Tatty whispered back. "What can I say?"

Then, as Mr. Not So Much made the first step out the door towards the rain, with a sudden burst of inspiration Tatty called after him: "Mr. Not So Much, what is the largest room in the world?"

He turned back, glowering in his usual dreadful way.

"Room for improvement, of course," he snapped. "Everyone knows that. And there's certainly plenty of it here!"

With that he banged the door shut behind him, and disappeared into the mist.

8

Tatty, Mary and Little Ann

"Room for improvement," Mr. Not So Much had said. The largest room in the world was room for improvement.

Tatty and Mary and Little Ann stared at each other, eyes round as plates, mouths fallen open with surprise. Now that they had the answer to the riddle, they were not sure they wanted it after all.

Miss Know It All was so nice, they wanted her to stay for ever. They had thought they would never really find the answer, and she would never go. But now she would be leaving.

72

And with her would go the beautiful picture of Albert.

And the silver music box.

And the wonderful box of chocolates.

Tatty and Mary and Little Ann looked at each other unhappily, and at last they were roused by the voices of the other girls as they came back down the hall from the kitchen.

Miss Plum came to the parlor doorway and stood surveying the boots and umbrellas without approval.

"I thought it was just a rainy day, but I think there's been a hurricane through this hall," she said.

Then she asked, "Can't these umbrellas be put to dry somewhere else?" But no one could think of anywhere else.

"Well, as soon as they are dry," she said, "see that they are furled and put back in the cupboard."

"Furled?" The biggest girl, Elsie May, put her hand over her mouth and giggled.

"Yes—furled," said Miss Plum. She caught

sight of Elsie May giggling. "You may be in charge of them, Elsie May."

That put Elsie May in her place. While the other girls went to play, she had to sit down on the stairway and wait until the umbrellas were dry. She sat and glowered at them.

"Come along—Tatty, Mary, Little Ann," Miss Plum called. "Why are you standing there by the door? Get out of those wet things."

"Yes, Miss Plum," Mary said, and Miss Plum went back into the parlor.

Very silently the three little girls took off their boots and lined them up along the edge of the carpet with the other boots. They had shared an umbrella to school, and Mary set this down to dry with the others.

"What does 'furled' mean?" Little Ann asked, but Tatty and Mary didn't answer because they were too busy thinking about what Mr. Not So Much had said.

Soberly they went down the hall to the kitchen. When they passed the parlor door, Miss Know It All happened to be looking up for a moment from writing down things she knew. She saw them and smiled and waved.

Tatty and Mary looked at each other, but they did not say a word. They hurried past the parlor doorway as fast as they could. Little Ann ran after them, and she did not say anything to Miss Know It All either.

And that night at supper not one little girl opened her mouth about the answer to the riddle. Not Tatty. Or Mary. Or Little Ann.

9

In the Parlor

Miss Know It All had never complained about having to stay so long at The Good Day. She had always remained cheerful. But on the very day that Mr. Not So Much gave Tatty and Mary and Little Ann the answer to the riddle, Miss Know It All at last found it almost too much to keep cheerful.

Perhaps it was the rain, drizzling down and splashing against the windows and into the puddles. Perhaps it was the thick soft grey mist filling the air ever more heavily as the dull afternoon drew to a close.

"I've drawn the green card," she murmured to herself, and Miss Plum and Miss Lavender asked her what she meant by that.

"It was a game I used to play when I was a child," Miss Know It All said. "It was called *Going Through Life*. You moved your marker round on a board—you know how games are." Miss Lavender and Miss Plum nodded. "If you drew a red card you moved six spaces, and if you drew a blue card you moved ten spaces. If you drew a white card you moved as far as it said; each white card said a different number. But if you drew a green card, you stayed right where you were. I feel I've drawn the whole stack of green cards at once."

And it seemed to do her no good at all to try to laugh about it.

But Miss Know It All kept on trying to be cheerful. That night when supper was over and the little girls came into the parlor, Miss Know It All passed round her wonderful refilling chocolate box. After they had eaten their chocolates, they were going to sing songs, and Miss Plum was already seated at the piano and Miss Lavender was tuning her violin.

"What shall we sing?" Miss Plum asked, and someone said, "Let's sing *In My House I Had a Dish*"—so Miss Plum began to play that. All the twenty-eight little girls sang as loudly as they could:

> *In my house I had a dish,*
> *And on the dish there was a fish,*
> *But he didn't see me!*

> *In my window I had a plant,*
> *And on the plant there was an ant,*
> *But he didn't see me!*

> *On my floor I had a rug,*
> *And on the rug there was a bug,*
> *But he didn't see me!*

The chocolate box had been passed all round, and Miss Know It All put on the cover and put the box back into her coat pocket. She was beginning to feel very sad again, and there were two tiny tears in the corners of her eyes.

The little girls went on singing:

> *On my table there was a pie,*
> *And on the pie was a butterfly,*
> *But he didn't see me!*

> *In my garden I had a tree,*
> *And on the tree there was a bee,*
> *But he didn't see me—I'M GLAD!*

As the girls were singing, Miss Lavender noticed that Miss Know It All did not look very happy. When the song was over at last, Miss Lavender said, "Dear Miss Know It All, don't feel so badly. We shall be happy to have you stay with us forever."

"Oh yes, yes!" All the girls began to chatter. But Miss Know It All shook her head, and the two tiny tears came into her eyes again.

"You've all been so kind," she said. "I can't think what a trouble I must be to you."

"Oh no, no, no," everyone cried.

"We don't want you to go, ever," Little Ann
said. Which was perfectly true; but after she had
said it she ran and hid her head in Mary's skirt,
because she knew the answer to the riddle.

"Why, whatever is the matter with Little
Ann?" Miss Plum said. She tried to tease Little

Ann and make her look out from Mary's skirt. But Little Ann would not look out.

"Miss Know It All is going to cry," Tatty whispered to Mary. They watched with fascination and alarm, for they had never seen anyone grown up cry before.

"Perhaps we'd better tell then," Mary whispered at last. "You go on, Tatty—it was your old question." Mary was feeling cross, because now Miss Know It All would leave, and Mary wanted her to stay forever.

Tatty went over to the sofa. Miss Know It All sniffed back her tears and dabbed at her nose with a handkerchief. "Don't mind me," she said. "I'm just a foolish old woman, crying like this—and it's not even Thursday. Thursday's the day to cry, if you've got to cry, my brother Albert always said."

"Is his name *Mr.* Know It All?" Elsie May asked.

Miss Know It All sniffed and dabbed at her nose and nodded. But she seemed to feel better, thinking of her brother. "Albert Know It All, " she said. "He was the handsomest man in our town.

He had a black moustache and shiny black shoes. He was a ladies' man, Albert was. And smart as a new pin. If he were to walk in right this minute, he'd know the largest room in the world." This made Miss Know It All feel sad again, to remember that she did not know.

"I know it," Tatty said—so softly that for a moment Miss Know It All was not sure she had heard correctly.

"I know it," Tatty said again, a little more

loudly. She couldn't stop now. She would have to tell. And Miss Know It All would leave.

"It's room for improvement," Tatty said. "Mr. Not So Much told us."

"Room for improvement!" Miss Know It All cried. And then she began to laugh and laugh and laugh. She shook all over, and tears poured from her eyes and down her face and splashed into her lap.

"Room for improvement!" cried Miss Plum, and she began to smile a little, and then a little more, and then a little more—until she was laughing too.

"Room for improvement!" cried Miss Lavender. "Oh my—oh my—oh my——" Then she began to laugh until all the fluffy white curls were bobbing on her head.

And all the little girls began to laugh, even Elsie May, who usually thought she was too fine to do what other people did. Even Tatty and Mary and Little Ann began to laugh, because they felt happy now that they had told the answer to the riddle. They had not felt very happy about having such a secret and not telling.

But Miss Know It All laughed the loudest and the longest and the merriest. At last, when she had recovered and mopped up her face, she said, "This means I must be on my way tomorrow."

"Oh—can't you stay a little longer?" everyone begged, but Miss Know It All shook her head firmly.

"Thank you anyway, but tomorrow I must be off. Why, I'm days behind schedule already. Think of the people all over the world I have not visited yet. Think of the questions they must be wanting to ask me. But never mind; after I've gone, I shall send you something to remember me by forever."

10

The Present

The next day the rain was over. The warm
spring sunshine filled Butterfield Square again,
and dried up all the puddles and all the muddy
spots where the new green spring grass was growing so fast. Lilac bushes were in bloom all along
the edge of the yard at Number 18. Cook had all
the kitchen windows open and lovely warm
breezes floated through, carrying all the good
smells on down the hall to the parlor.

Miss Know It All stood in the hall by the front
door, as fresh and neat as the day she came. The
twenty-eight girls came filing out of the dining

room, where they had just finished their breakfast. They were very quiet, for it was a solemn moment. They were all going to miss Miss Know It All, and they were also wondering what present she was going to send them. ("A picture of herself, I bet," Elsie May had told the girls. "That's the thing that will make us remember her forever.")

"Well, you've got a good day for starting out," Miss Plum said.

"Of course," said Miss Know It All—as if she had known all along that it would be a nice day.

Then she said, "If I had time, I would let you all have a turn at asking questions. But I am so behind schedule—I'm sure you all understand."

"Oh, we all understand," Miss Lavender said. "Anyway, I don't think we have any questions left to ask."

"Well then, it's time I was on my way," Miss Know It All said.

Miss Plum opened the door, and Miss Know It All waved to everyone one last time and stepped smartly along the pavement by the black iron railings. Even then Little Ann thought Miss Know It All might just for fun turn the railings into real licorice as she passed—but she only walked along the road in a very ordinary way and turned to wave back to everyone once more.

"Goodbye, goodbye," they all called to her. They watched her until she was out of sight down the street.

Miss Lavender looked very wistful, and Miss Plum cleared her throat and clapped her hands together and said, "Now, now. Let's not stand around moping. Coats and books; time for school."

Off to school ran the little girls, one by one, two by two, three by three, all strung out, coats flying in the warm spring wind. They were sorry Miss Know It All was gone—but perhaps she would come back some day. And in the meantime, she was going to send them a present, and they would remember her forever.

Little Ann felt the black iron railings to see if they were still only iron, and they were. They were very smooth and hard and cool against her

fingers, not soft and sticky, as licorice would
be . . . and then she ran to catch up with the
others.

Two days later a square brown-paper package
came in the post to Number 18 Butterfield Square.
It was addressed to Miss Plum and Miss Lavender
and Cook—*and:*

Tatty and Mary and Little Ann,
Frannie and Phoebe and Flora Suzanne;

Sophie and Sally,
Nonnie and Nellie,
Clara and Agnes, Margie and Jane,
Penny and Polly,
Dora and Dolly,
Kitty and Kate and Elaine;

Emmy and Cissie, Elizabeth, Sue,
Bonnie and Wendy and Elsie May, too.

Inside the package was a small book with a
blue velvet cover and a title made of gold. The title
said: *Never-ending Stories.*

The Present

A letter from Miss Know It All fluttered out when the package was unwrapped. Miss Plum opened the letter and began to read it aloud to all the girls, who listened eagerly.

"Every time you open this book there will be a new story to read. You can never wear it out. It is guaranteed forever."

"Let's see—let's see," the girls began to clamour, before Miss Plum could even finish the letter.

So Miss Plum opened the book and read the name of the story aloud. *The Enchanted Prince of the Dark Mountain.*

She turned the book so that everyone could see the picture of the handsome prince in his red cape and tall boots. Behind him loomed the dark and mysterious mountain.

"Once upon a time, in a faraway land, there lived a prince——" Miss Plum began to read. Then she stopped and looked at Miss Lavender. Miss Lavender nodded. All the girls held their breath. Solemnly Miss Plum closed the book. She waited a moment, looking round at the girls, and then she opened it again.

Now the picture showed an old witch with streaming black hair, carrying a pig under her arm. All the people of the town had their heads stuck out of the windows of their shops and houses to watch as she went by. The name of this story was *The Witch's Secret*.

"Once upon a time," Miss Plum read, "there lived a stingy old witch who would not give a penny to anyone——" The handsome prince of the dark mountain was gone forever.

"We must be careful not to lose our stories before we've read them," Miss Plum said, and she put the book down very carefully, face up, wide open. Miss Lavender put her letter opener across the pages so that the book would not close by accident before they had found out the secret of the stingy old witch who would not give a penny away.

Then Miss Plum continued with Miss Know It All's letter:

The Present

"*You must be careful to finish each story before you close the book.*" (Everyone laughed for now they knew that already!) "*I hope you will like this book, and I hope you will never forget*
        Your friend,

Miss Know It All

P.S. I know I shall never forget you."